The Dinosaur's Packed Lunch

Dinah crept away, feeling very empty. She wandered back to the iguanodon, sucking her thumb.

"I wish I had a mum to make me a packed lunch," said Dinah.

A hand reached out and patted her on the shoulder.

A huge scaly hand with a spiked thumb!

The Dinosaur's Packed Lunch

The Dinosaur's Packed Lunch

Jacqueline Wilson

Illustrated by Nick Sharratt

THE DINOSAUR'S PACKED LUNCH
A CORGI PUPS BOOK 978 0 552 55782 5

First published in Great Britain by Doubleday,
an imprint of Random House Children's Books
A Random House Group Company

Doubleday edition published 1995
First Corgi Pups edition published 1996
This Corgi Pups edition published 2008

1 3 5 7 9 10 8 6 4 2

Text copyright © Jacqueline Wilson, 1995
Illustrations copyright © Nick Sharratt, 1996

The Random House Group Limited makes every effort to ensure that the papers used in its books
are made from trees that have been legally sourced from well-managed and credibly certified forests.
Our paper procurement policy can be found at: www.randomhouse.co.uk/paper.htm

Mixed Sources
Product group from well-managed
forests and other controlled sources
www.fsc.org Cert no. TT-COC-2139
© 1996 Forest Stewardship Council
FSC

Set in Monotype Bembo Schoolbook

Young Corgi Books are published by Random House Children's Books,
61–63 Uxbridge Road, London W5 5SA

www.**kids**at**randomhouse**.co.uk
www.**rbooks**.co.uk

Addresses for companies within The Random House Group Limited can be found at:
www.randomhouse.co.uk/offices.htm

THE RANDOM HOUSE GROUP Limited Reg. No. 954009

A CIP catalogue record for this book is available from the British Library.

Printed in the UK by CPI Bookmarque, Croydon, CR0 4TD

For Bunny, with lots of love

CONTENTS

Series Reading Consultant: Prue Goodwin
Reading and Language Information Centre,
University of Reading

Chapter One

Dinah woke up early.

She didn't feel like getting washed. She didn't feel like getting dressed. She didn't feel like going to school.

"Boring," said Dinah.

Dinah did not feel like
breakfast.

Not cornflakes and milk.

"Boring," said Dinah.

She made herself a jam
sandwich.

"Yummy," said Dinah,
rubbing her tummy.

She fed the teddy on her
nightie, too.

Dinah wanted a drink but the
lemonade was right at the top of
the cupboard with Dad's beer.

Dinah couldn't reach.

Then she saw Dad's window-
cleaning ladder.

Dinah nearly reached the
lemonade.

But then the ladder slipped.

Dad woke up early, too.

Dinah hated it when Dad got cross. She didn't have a mum or any brothers or sisters. Dinah just had her dad.

"How am I going to clean the windows now?" said Dad. "And take that thumb out of your mouth, baby."

Dinah always sucked her thumb when she was sad. Her special sucking thumb was starting to get a bit pointed.

Dinah was still sucking her
thumb when she went to school.
The boys teased her. Dinah got
cross. There was a fight.

Then Miss Smith got cross and
sent Dinah indoors.

Dinah had a little wash.
Dinah's best friend, Judy,
ended up having a little wash,
too.

Miss Smith got very cross and said Dinah wouldn't go on the school trip to the museum if she wasn't careful.

"A museum?" Dinah muttered. "Boring."

Dinah's best friend, Judy, was still very damp. She didn't feel like sitting next to Dinah on the minibus. She sat next to Danielle, and they kept giggling together.

Dinah had to sit next to Miss Smith.

When they got to the museum
Judy went off arm in arm with
Danielle.

"I don't care," said Dinah,
sucking her thumb.

13

Chapter Two

Dinah cheered up when they went into a special dinosaur exhibition. Dinosaurs were huge monsters who lived millions of years ago.

Dinah liked the look of dinosaurs.

Some of the dinosaurs were very fierce and vicious. Judy and Danielle squealed. Dinah didn't mind a bit.

The dinosaurs had huge long names to match their size.

Dinah wasn't very good at reading but she found she had no problem spelling out brontosaurus . . .

. . . and tyrannosaurus and triceratops.

She particularly liked the
iguanodon. It had a funny
pointed thumb spike. Perhaps the
iguanodon sucked
its thumb, too.

Miss Smith got cross because
Dinah kept lagging behind.

"Hurry up, Dinah. It's
lunchtime," said Miss Smith.

Everyone had a packed lunch
except Dinah. Dad always
forgot things like packed lunches.
Sometimes Judy shared her
packed lunch with Dinah. But
not today.

"Ooh, my mum's given me
prawn sandwiches and a bunch
of grapes and a Kit Kat and a
can of Coke. Want half my
Kit Kat, Danielle?" said Judy.

Dinah crept away, feeling
very empty. She wandered back
to the iguanodon, sucking her
thumb.

"I wish I had a mum to make
me a packed lunch," said Dinah.

IGUANODON

A hand reached out and
patted her on the shoulder.

A huge scaly hand with a
spiked thumb!

The iguanodon reached down
and picked Dinah up. It cradled
her in its arms, rocking
backwards and forwards.

The iguanodon made Dinah
her own packed lunch.

She ate a leaf sandwich, a
bunch of daisies, a twig snack
bar and a bottle of dinosaur
juice.

The dinosaur juice was a very bright green. It tasted strange too, but Dinah drank a few drops.

The iguanodon wiped Dinah's mouth in a motherly way.

"Dinah! Where *are* you?"

Miss Smith was coming! Dinah jumped down and the iguanodon shot back into place with a rattle and a clunk. Miss Smith didn't see. She was cross with Dinah.

Dinah was too dazed to care.

All the other children were in
the gift shop buying books and
stickers and little rubber
dinosaurs.

Dinah didn't have any money
but she didn't mind. She didn't
want a book or a sticker or a
little rubber dinosaur.

She had just had a dinosaur's
packed lunch!

Dinah was very quiet on the bus going back.

"You're not going to be sick, are you, Dinah?" Miss Smith asked anxiously.

Dinah wasn't sure. She felt very strange. She sucked her thumb, but it tasted strange, too.

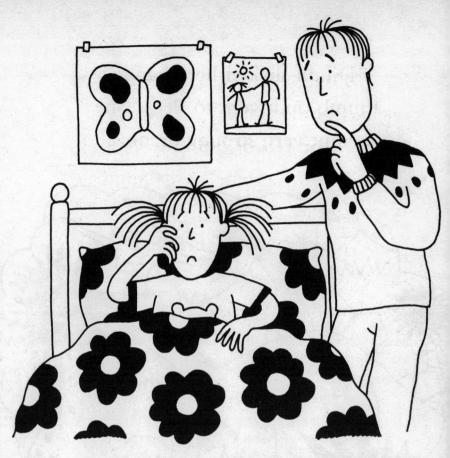

She went to bed straight after
supper. Perhaps she should have
had a bath. Her skin felt strange
now, hard and dry and itchy.

Dinah sucked her strange
thumb and went to sleep. She
dreamt very strange dreams.

Chapter Three

When Dinah woke, something
even stranger had happened.

She sat up and her head
bumped against the ceiling! Her
bed was so tiny she had to cram
her knees right up under her
chin.

Her bedroom had shrunk in
the night.

No. Even stranger . . .

Dinah had grown. She had
grown and grown and grown.
She had grown a long back and
long legs and a long tail!

Dinah gasped and sucked her thumb. At least she still *had* a thumb.

She wondered what to do.

She decided she'd better tell Dad.

She had to bend double to
get out of her bedroom door
and . . .

edge along the hall, her head
neatly sweeping up the cobwebs
(Dinah and her dad didn't
bother about dusting) . . .

and then she had to bend right
down again to get into Dad's
bedroom.

"Dad. Dad! Wake up, Dad,"
said Dinah.

"What's the matter?" Dad
mumbled. "Stop yelling at me,
Dinah."

Dad peered out from under
the bedcovers. He saw Dinah.

Dad was the one who did the
yelling this time.

"Aaaaaaaaah!"

"A monster! A monster! Run, Dinah, there's a monster in my bedroom," Dad yelled.

"Hey, Dad. It's me, Dinah. I'm the monster," said Dinah. "Well, I think I've turned into a dinosaur, actually. It feels a bit scary. Give me a cuddle, Dad."

It was a bit scary for Dad, too. But he could see the huge dinosaur in his bedroom was wearing Dinah's nightie and talking with Dinah's voice.

It was his daughter Dinah all right. So he gave her a cuddle as best he could.

Then Dinah gave Dad a
cuddle, which was much easier.
It was fun being able to pick
Dad up with her new arms.
She'd have to remember to cut
her claws though.

Her new skin didn't need a
wash but her arms ached when
she cleaned all her new teeth
with Dad's big clothes-brush.

Dinah was terribly greedy at breakfast. She ate a whole loaf of bread in one gollop and finished a jar of jam with one lick.

"Well, I'm a growing girl," said Dinah, giggling.

"I don't know how I'm going to afford to feed you now. Money doesn't grow on trees," said Dad.

Luckily, Dinah liked eating trees. Well, the leaves and the smaller snappier branches. And privet hedges taste delicious if you're a dinosaur.

Everyone got their hedges trimmed and their trees pruned for nothing.

Chapter Four

Dad took Dinah to the doctor's.

"Can you cure my Dinah?" asked Dad.

"I think you'd better take her to a vet," said the doctor.

Dinah did a bit of doctoring
herself.

She cured a baby's hiccups
and made an old lady's bad leg
better.

45

Dad took Dinah to the vet's.
"Well, she's certainly got a
healthy appetite," said the vet.
"I don't think there's anything
wrong with her."

"In that case you'd better go
to school," said Dad.

"Boring," said Dinah.

But maybe school might be
more fun today.

She certainly caused a bit of
fuss when she went in through
the school gates.

Dad had to have a few words
with Miss Smith.

Miss Smith wasn't at all sure
she could cope with this new
Dinah.

"It's OK, Miss Smith. I'll be
ever so good," said Dinah.

Dinah did try to be good. She didn't talk in the (now very crowded) class, but when she started to get bored she gave her new long tail a little flick . . .

which caused a bit of bother . . .

and at playtime she fought the
boys . . .

and splashed the girls BUT . . . .

she somehow didn't get into
trouble.

Everyone wanted to play with Dinah now.

"Dinah's my best friend," said Judy.

"I'll be best friends with everyone," said Dinah. "Hey, who wants a ride on my tail?"

"Dinah's better than
Disneyland!" said Judy.

Dinah even gave Miss Smith a
ride!

When Dad collected her from
school, Dinah helped him clean
all the windows in the street.

People paid double
to watch Dad
climb up and
down his new
ladder.

Dinah and Dad got very hot
working so hard.

"Let's go home and have a
cool bath," said Dad.

"Boring," said Dinah. "Let's
go swimming."

So Dinah and Dad went to
the swimming pool. There
wasn't much pool left after
Dinah dived in!

Dinah made an excellent
diving board and water fountain.

It took Dad a very long time
to get her properly dry.

Dad had fish and chips for
supper.

Dinah had leaves and privet
and dandelions and nettles and
long grass and a big bunch of
flowers *and* fish and chips.

"Yummy," said Dinah,
rubbing her tummy.

Dad tried his best to tuck her
up in bed.

Dinah sucked her new spiked
thumb until she fell asleep
and . . .

when she woke up she was a
little girl again.

"Boring," said Dinah.

But she still had a nearly full
bottle of dinosaur juice . . .

THE END

ABOUT THE AUTHOR

JACQUELINE WILSON is one of Britain's most
outstanding writers for young readers. She is the
most borrowed author from British libraries and
has sold over 25 million books in this country.
As a child, she always wanted to be a writer and
wrote her first 'novel' when she was nine, filling
countless exercise books as she grew up. She started
work at a publishing company and then went on
to work as a journalist on *Jackie* magazine (which
was named after her) before turning to writing
fiction full-time.

Jacqueline has been honoured with many
of the UK's top awards for children's books,
including the Guardian Children's Fiction
Award, the Smarties Prize, the Red House Book
Award and the Children's Book of the Year.
She was awarded an OBE in 2002 and was
the Children's Laureate for 2005-2007.

ABOUT THE ILLUSTRATOR

NICK SHARRATT knew from an early age that
he wanted to use his drawing skills as his career,
so he went to Manchester Polytechnic to do an
Art Foundation course. He followed this up with
a BA (Hons) in Graphic Design at St. Martin's
School of Art in London from 1981–1984.

Since graduating, Nick has been working full-time
as an illustrator for children's books, publishers and
a wide range of magazines. His brilliant illustrations
have brought to life many books, most notably
the titles by Jacqueline Wilson.

Nick also writes books as well as illustrating them.

THE MONSTER STORY–TELLER
Jacqueline Wilson

"Monster Planet, here we come!"

One morning at school, Natalie is feeling bored
– until a tiny monster waves at her from a plant
on the classroom window sill. The monster
whizzes her off in his mini flying saucer for
some MONSTER FUN. Now Natalie really
has some monster stories to tell!

An exciting and funny adventure
from the award-winning author of
The Dinosaur's Packed Lunch.

ISBN: 978 0 552 55787 0

LIZZIE ZIPMOUTH
Jacqueline Wilson

"Why don't you ever say anything, Lizzie?"
said Rory. "It's like you've got a zip
across your mouth."

Lizzie refuses to speak.

She doesn't want to talk to Rory or Jake, her new
stepbrothers, or Sam, their dad, or even her mum.
She's totally fed up at having to join a new family
and nothing can coax her into speaking to them.
Not football, not pizza, not a new bedroom.
That is, until she meets a member of the new
family who is even more stubborn than her -
and has had a lot more practice!

ISBN: 978 0 552 55784 9

SLEEPOVERS
Jacqueline Wilson

Sleepover parties are the greatest!
Everybody's having one . . .

All of Daisy's friends in the Alphabet Club – Amy,
Bella, Chloe and Emily, have had sleepovers for their
birthdays. Daisy has a dilemma. She'd love to have a
sleepover too, but then she'd have to let her
friends meet her sister…

A funny and moving story for younger readers
from the award-winning author of *Lizzie Zipmouth*
and *Double Act*.

ISBN: 978 0 552 55783 2

THE MUM-MINDER
Jacqueline Wilson

"I'm Sadie and I'm nearly nine. Mum's a
childminder, but she doesn't have to mind me.
I can mind myself, easy-peasy. Lucky for Mum,
because now she's got the flu, so I've got to
mind her - and help with all the babies!"

A hilarious, entertaining and lively account,
told throughout in Sadie's own words, of one
chaotic week in the life of a young girl whose
mother is a childminder.

ISBN: 978 0 440 86825 5